丁丁企鵝遊學館

閱亮點
ENRICH SPOT

丁丁企鵝遊學館

有情有境學英語

02 日常篇 Daily Life

原作 江記 · 撰文 閱亮點編輯室

Contents
目錄

Meet the characters
角色介绍

Ding Ding
A little penguin.
He is a lively kid
who is ready to play
at all times!

Mum
Ding Ding's mother.
She always teaches
Ding Ding to be
a well-behaved child.

Dad
Ding Ding's father.
He loves his family
so much.

Mushroom

A friend of Ding Ding.
Her hairstyle makes her
look like a mushroom!

Glasses

Another friend.
He always wears
a pair of glasses.

Ryan

Ding Ding's cousin.
He is a mature penguin
for his age.

Masihung

A bear who wears a mask on his face.
He goes beyond lazy and
into super lazy!

Panda

A roommate of Masihung.
He is a conscientious panda. Sadly,
he is worlds apart from Masihung.

Getting up 起牀

The alarm clock goes off. Time to get up.

Yawn...

1 Alarm clock 鬧鐘

2 Goes off 大聲響起

3 Rise and shine! 打起精神，快起牀！

Have you slept well?

Rise and shine!

Good morning.

Brushing the teeth 刷牙

1 Squeeze 擠壓

2 Toothpaste 牙膏

3 Well done. 做得好。

Going to the toilet 上廁所

1. Pee 小便
2. Poo 大便
3. It stinks! 好臭啊！
4. Toot 呠呠（放屁的聲音）

Flushing the toilet 沖廁所

1 Forget 忘記

2 Bathroom 洗手間

3 Close the lid 關上廁板

Taking a bath 洗澡

1 Bath 洗澡 / 浴缸

2 Fishing 釣魚

Ready to go 出門

1 Ready 準備

2 Hang on. 等一等。

Back home 回家

Bedtime story 睡前故事

> Mum, can you read me a story?

1 One moment. 等一會。

2 Awake 醒着

> One moment. Mummy's coming... Hey, are you still awake?

> Knock!
>
> Knock!

Going to the bed 上牀睡覺

It's late now.
Time to go to the bed!

I'm not tired yet.

Sleepy boy, do you know what time is it? It's bedtime already.

Let's check it out.

1 Late 夜深

2 Check it out 了解一下

Having breakfast 吃早餐

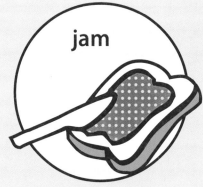

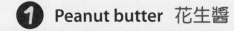

1 Peanut butter 花生醬

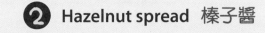

2 Hazelnut spread 榛子醬

1 Mouth-watering 令人垂涎欲滴

2 Delicious 美味

What dessert is this?
這是甚麼甜品？

This is a roll cake.

I'll do a magic for you.

See. This is a lollipop now.

What a tasty magic!

Ha-ha!

1 Magic 魔術

2 Lollipop 波板糖

Mealtime 吃飯時間

1. Dig in 開始吃
2. Belch 打嗝
3. Full 飽了

Picky eater 挑吃鬼

1 Vegetable 蔬菜

2 Picky 挑剔

3 No way! 不要啊！

Drinking 喝飲品

1 Gulp 大口地喝

2 Yuck! 唷！（表示反感的聲音）

3 Awful 糟糕

4 Potion 魔藥

5 Witch 女巫

Sweeping the floor 掃地

1 Smell a rat 有可疑

2 Rubbish 垃圾

Vacuuming up 吸塵

1 Leave me alone. 不要打擾我。

2 Speck of dust 微塵

Kitchen time 煮食時間

1 Give me a hand 幫幫我

2 Go for it! 去吧！（表示激勵）

Cleaning up 收拾

Can I help cleaning up the table?

Certainly.

① Certainly. 當然可以。

② Such 真的是

It's done, Mum.

You did a great job. Thank you for the help. You're such a good boy.

Washing the dishes 洗碗碟

1. Take turns 輪流
2. Superhero 超級英雄
3. Clank 噹（發出金屬碰撞的聲音）

Making the bed 整理牀鋪

1 Mess 髒亂

2 Tidy up 整理、收拾

3 A bit 一會兒

What to wear 穿甚麼好

1 Wear 穿

2 Decide 決定

Getting dressed 穿衣服

1 Get dressed yourself
自己穿衣

2 Put on 穿上

We're going out today.
Can you get dressed yourself?

OK. I'll put my shirt on.

O-oh!

A pair of socks? 一雙襪子？

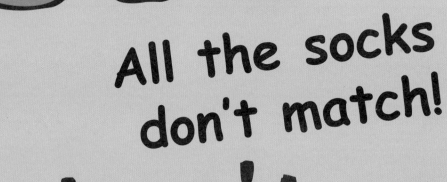

1 Match 配對

2 Check out 查看一下

Doing the laundry 洗衣服

1 Snooze 打瞌睡

2 Finish 完成

3 Take a nap 小睡片刻

Sorting clothes 整理衣物

1 Fold 摺疊

2 Give it a try 試一試

3 Why not? 好啊。

4 Oh, my! 噢，天啊！

Looking after a pet 照顧寵物

1 So do I. 我也是。

2 Relaxed 輕鬆的

On the phone 聽電話

Hello.

Sorry.
He's out.

Hello, this is Ding Ding.
May I speak to Glasses?

I'm sure you ARE Glasses.
You just pretend you were not!

1 Out 外出、不在

2 Pretend 假裝

Sick 生病

1 Dizzy 暈

2 Have a temperature 發燒

3 Go to the doctor 看病

Taking the medicine 吃藥

I can't stop sneezing and coughing.

Cough!

Here, take the medicine.

No!
It tastes terrible.

1 ACHOO! 乞嗤！
（打噴嚏的聲音）

2 Sneeze 打噴嚏

3 Cough 咳嗽

4 Terrible 糟糕

丁丁企鵝遊學館

有情有境
學英語 **02** 日常篇 Daily Lif

原作	江記（江康泉）
撰文	閱亮點編輯室
內容總監	曾玉英
責任編輯	Zeny Lam & Hockey Yeung
顧問編輯	Pray Eucha
書籍設計	Stephen Chan

出版	閱亮點有限公司 Enrich Spot Limited
	九龍觀塘鴻圖道 78 號 17 樓 A 室
發行	天窗出版社有限公司 Enrich Publishing Ltd.
	九龍觀塘鴻圖道 78 號 17 樓 A 室
電話	(852) 2793 5678
傳真	(852) 2793 5030
網址	www.enrichculture.com
電郵	info@enrichculture.com
出版日期	2021 年 7 月初版

承印	嘉昱有限公司
	九龍新蒲崗大有街 26-28 號天虹大廈 7 字樓

定價	港幣 $88　新台幣 $440
國際書號	978-988-75704-2-4
圖書分類	(1) 兒童圖書　　(2) 英語學習

ding_ding_penguin